A Doubleday Book for Young Readers

Published by
Random House, Inc.
1540 Broadway
New York, New York 10036

Doubleday and the portrayal of an anchor with a dolphin are trademarks of Random House, Inc.

First American edition 1999
First published in Great Britain by Orion Children's Books 1999

Library of Congress Cataloging-in-Publication Data
ISBN: 0-385-32683-1
Cataloging-in-Publication Data is available from the U.S. Library of Congress.

The text of this book is set in 18-point Palatino.

Manufactured in Italy

November 1999

10 9 8 7 6 5 4 3 2 1

MY FAVORITE WORD BOOK

Words and Pictures
for the Very Young

SELINA YOUNG

A Doubleday Book for Young Readers

Pat the cat

Patch the dog

Smudge the rabbit

Ladybug that was just passing

fire station

shops

airport

movie theater

construction site

park

sidewalk

Town

road

hospital

school

factory

gas station

train

train station

library

dentist's office

trash can

house

hotel

traffic circle

streetlamp

7

Travel

balloon

bus

motorcycle

airplane

bike

ship

I can't find Patch and Smudge, can you?

submarine

8

playhouse

blocks

chairs

table

painting

sandbox

blackboard

chalk

dress-up box

friends

teacher

School

Welcome to our school Olivia

How many paintings can you count?

crayons
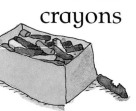

paint

books

toilets

globe

scissors

apron

numbers

1 7 9

playground

The little red hen went cluck, cluck, cluck!

boy

girl

lunch box

j W r

letters

tape player

pegs

clock

computer

pencils

glue

paper

water

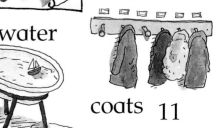

coats

11

eyebrow

eye

hair

teeth

ear

mouth

neck

chin

shoulder

heel

hand

fingernail

knee

thumb

leg

ankle

nose

face

stomach

13

doctor

nurse

What day is it today?

teacher

Jobs

ballet dancer

computer operator

farmer

actor

hairdresser

dentist

photographer

soccer player

truck driver

14

firefighter

fisher

builder

mechanic

acrobat

clown

shopkeeper

singer

chef

astronaut

What will you be, Toby?

15

Car

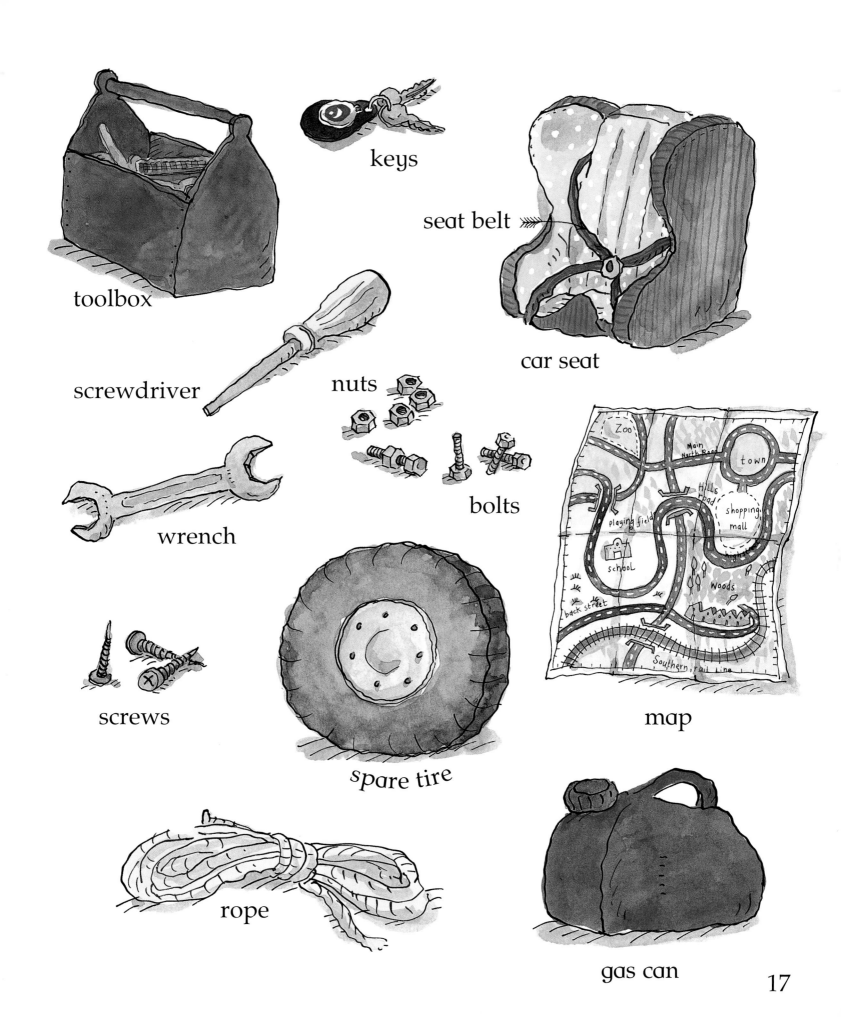

toolbox

keys

seat belt

car seat

screwdriver

nuts

bolts

wrench

screws

spare tire

map

rope

gas can

17

House

Housework

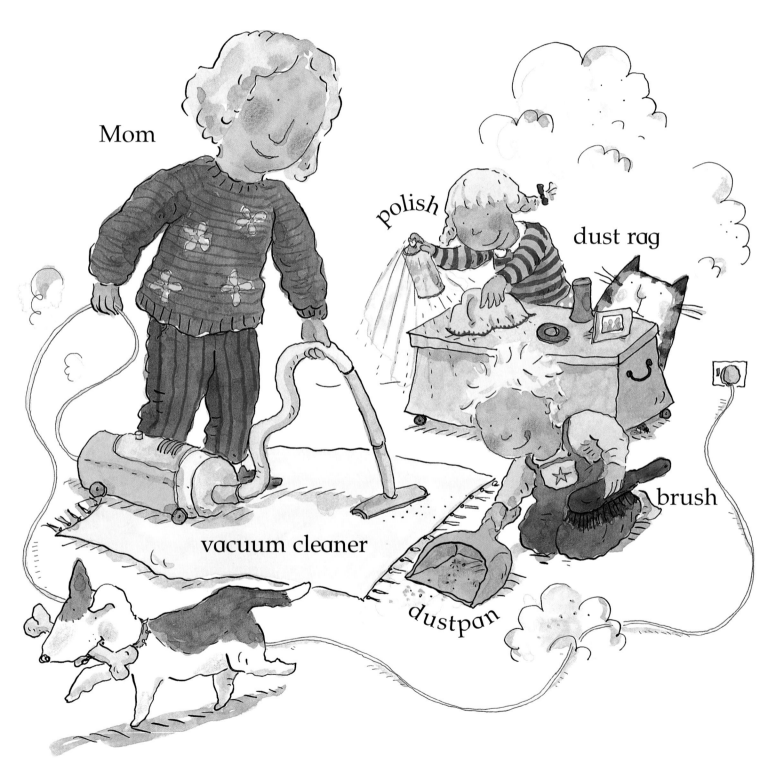

Mom

polish

dust rag

vacuum cleaner

brush

dustpan

farmer
hello
eggs
henhouse
hen
cockadoodledooo
chicks
rooster
doghouse
woof
dog
quack
duck
ducklings
pond
calf
cow
bull
barn

Farm

How many sheep can you count?

pig
pigsty
piglet

22

Vehicles

tow truck

forklift

steamroller

crane

cement mixer

car carrier

gas tanker

steam shovel

dump truck

bulldozer

Which one would you like to drive?

Birthday

Jell-O

sandwiches

sausages on sticks

popcorn

balloons

streamers

camera

friends

presents

birthday cards

chips

Happy Birthday to you

How many cookies are left?

Happy Birthday

I am 4

Happy Birthday

Zoe

26

wrapping paper

cake

candles

plate

straw

cups

party hat

cupcakes

cookies

spoon

27

necklace

thread

beads

face paints

board game

tea set

dollhouse

puzzle

finger puppets

horse

Sit up, dolly.

comb

stroller

29

Department Store

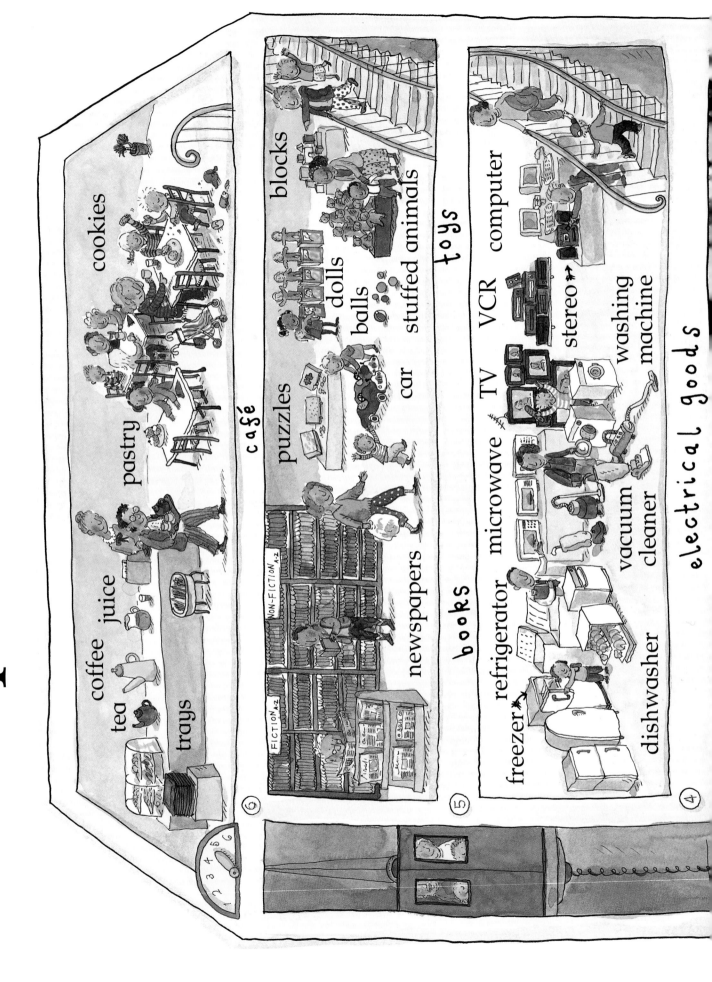

café — cookies · pastry · coffee · juice · tea · trays

books — blocks · puzzles · dolls · balls · car · stuffed animals · newspapers
NON-FICTION A–Z · FICTION A–Z

toys

electrical goods — computer · stereo · microwave · TV · VCR · washing machine · refrigerator · vacuum cleaner · freezer · dishwasher

31

Clothing

socks

sun hat

undershirt

underpants

scarf

tights

shirt

hairband

T-shirt

skirt

pants

bathing suit

dress

coat

sneakers

shoes

When it's hot, I like wearing my bathing suit.

sweatshirt

cap

winter hat

belt

gloves

bathrobe

nightgown

sweater

pajamas

When it's cold, we bundle up warm.

shorts

leotard

cardigan

ribbon

boots

patch

33

Cake

Mom

apron

bowl

Yummy! I like baking.

oven

wooden spoon

baking pan

scale

mixer

recipe

flour

sieve

oven mitts

eggs

sugar

salt

chocolate
buttons

butter

whisk

pitcher

timer

frosting

plate

crumbs

knife

cake

35

Play

merry-go-round

children

sandbox

book

basketball

soccer ball

tennis

Rollerblades

music

xylophone

hopscotch

CHALK

36

monkey bars

swings

tent

slide

seesaw

skateboard

bike

cards

I'm playing hide-and-seek with Patch and Pat. Can you help me find them?

37

beach chair

sun hat

sunscreen

picnic

shells

sailboarder

38

sand castle

sand

waves

sea

starfish

beach

Seaside

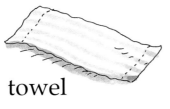
towel

flag

boat

cliffs

crab

buoy

seaweed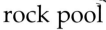

rock pool

shovel

bucket

bathing suit

trunks

umbrella

sunglasses

How many seagulls can you count?

lifeguard

kite

seagull

armbands

people

39

Animals

chimpanzee

snake

giraffe

tiger

I live in India.

lion

crocodile

zebra

elephant

I'm strong.

parrot

rhinoceros

leopard

kangaroo

bear

hippopotamus

wolf

panda

antelope

camel

penguin

gorilla

polar bear

ostrich

41

Supermarket

jars

cookies

jam

bottles

tea

coffee

pasta

flour

sugar

juice

FRUITS and VEGETABLES

bananas

cucumbers

onions

oranges

apples

lettuce

carrots

chips

lemons

potatoes

tomatoes

42

43

Food

milk

bread

yogurt

apple

cheese

orange

chocolate

spaghetti

pasta shapes

toast

butter

jam

baked beans

burger

sausages

fish sticks

grapes

ice cream

ice cream bar

strawberries

candy

44

French fries
ketchup

chips

raisins

cookies

orange juice

pancakes
syrup

salt and pepper

eggs

pizza

hot chocolate

honey

cake

corn

I love pizza. Do you?

45

Painting

crayons

handprints

paper

tissue paper

picture

paint

water jar

markers

glue

glitter

apron

scissors

string

paintbrushes

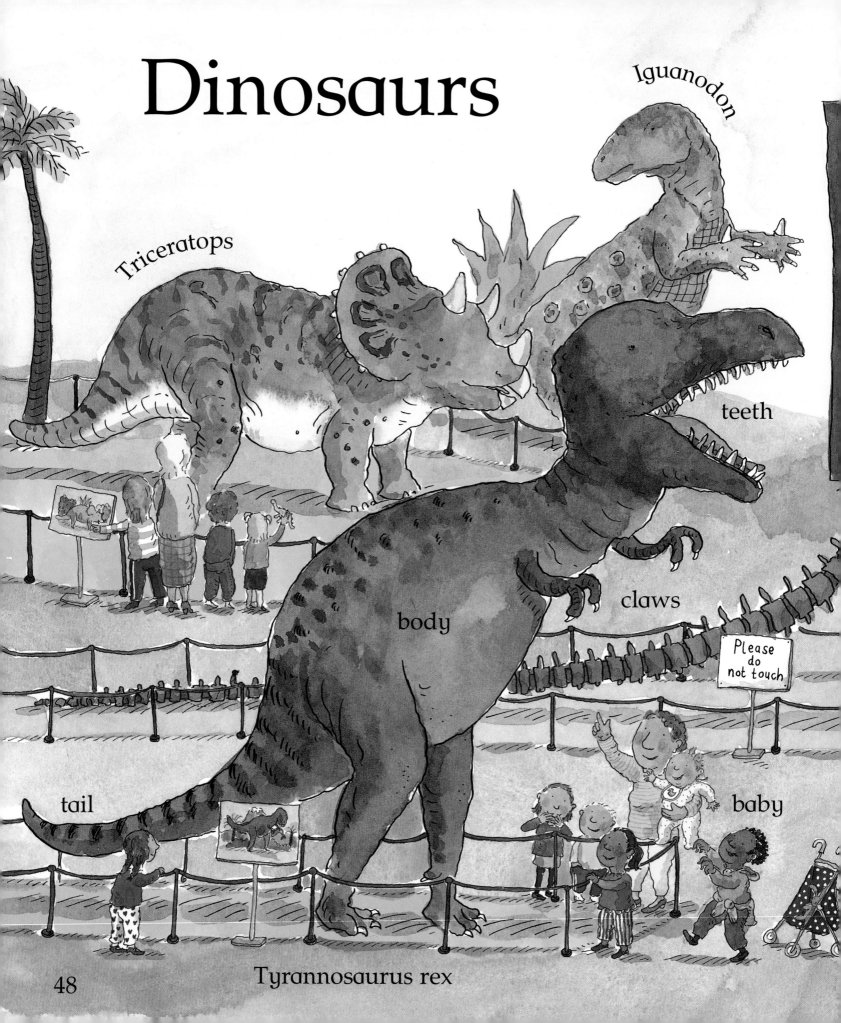

Dinosaurs

Iguanodon

Triceratops

teeth

claws

body

Please do not touch

tail

baby

Tyrannosaurus rex

48

 flowerpots

 snail

grass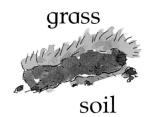

soil

worm

butterfly

 weeds

 bird

 fork

 tree

petals daisy

Garden

 50 watering can

 sunflower

 bee

pond

frog

rake

fence

branches

leaves

gate

flowers

flower bed

How many flowerpots can you count?

nest

hedge

peas

shed

Do you like playing in the garden?

vegetable patch

tomatoes

lettuce

caterpillar

51

Pets

guinea pig

mice

gerbil

hamster

lizard

Look, Toby, your fish is eating all the fish food.

cat

dog

goldfish

canary

puppy

kitten

rabbit

turtle

pony

mouse

53

Swimming Pool

slide

lifeguard

Lifeguard

life preserver

goggles

bathing cap

kickboard

lockers

Watch me! I'm going to dive in.

NO RUNNING OR PUSHING

diving board

DEEP END

water

towel

armbands

bathing suit

55

shark

octopus

anchor

swordfish

seahorse

coral

diver

turtle

eel

57

Music

orchestra

trumpet

triangle

handbells

drum

violin

bow

recorder

tambourine

guitar

music

cymbals

piano

59

Amusement Park

Ferris wheel

train

cave

ghost

dragon

fairy

fairy forest

king

knight

ENTRANCE

Howdy!

Hello!

ticket

alien

60

cowboy

Book

page

book

bookmark

Jack and the Beanstalk

The Three Little Pigs

Snow White and the Seven Dwarfs

Cinderella

Little Red Riding Hood

63

stars

bat

woof

toothbrush

pajamas

toothpaste

book

pillow

lamp

blanket

curtain

MAIL

Smudge

64